THIRD GRADE

ANGELS

THIRD GRADE

GRADE

ANGELS

BY JERRY SPINELLI

ILLUSTRATIONS BY JENNIFER A. BELL

Arthur A. Levine Books

An Imprint of Scholastic Inc.

Library of Congress Cataloging-in-Publication Data

Spinelli, Jerry.
Third grade angels / by Jerry Spinelli ; illustrations by
Jennifer A. Bell. — 1st ed.
p. cm.
Summary: "George 'Suds' Morton competes with his third-grade
classmates to earn the first 'halo' of the year for good behavior, but being
good turns out to be more stressful than he anticipated" —
Provided by publisher.
ISBN 978-0-545-38772-9 (hardback) [1. Friendship — Fiction. 2. Conduct
of life — Fiction. 3. Schools — Fiction.] I. Bell, Jennifer (Jennifer A.),
1977– ill. II. Title.
PZ7.S75663Thi 2012
[Fic]　dc23
2012001979

10 9 8 7 6 5 4 3 2 1　12 13 14 15 16

Printed in the U.S.A.　23

First edition, September 2012

Book design by Kristina Iulo
Art Direction by Elizabeth B. Parisi

To Lorna and Lou

MAY 16, 1936

TABLE OF CONTENTS

1

FINALLY!

I heard it first in kindergarten:

First grade babies!
Second grade cats!
Third grade angels!
Fourth grade rats!

I didn't like being a first-grade baby. (I wasn't a baby.)

I didn't like being a second-grade cat. (I like dogs.)

All this time I've been waiting to be an angel — and now I am! Today was the first day of third grade.

We could see it from the hallway as we headed for our new classroom. It was right on the door, a big sign:

WELCOME ANGELS

Our new teacher, Mrs. Simms, was standing there saying it to each of us as we entered the classroom:

"Welcome, angel Brett . . ."

"Welcome, angel Heather . . ."

"Welcome, angel Emma . . ."

Amazing! How did she know our names already? She shook each student's hand.

When it was my turn, she shook my hand and said, "Welcome, angel George."

Only my teachers call me George. My real name is Suds.

When we were all in our seats, Mrs. Simms gave us the biggest smile I've ever seen. I knew right away that we were the best class she ever had. I fired my best smile back at her.

She held out her arms. "Good morning, angels!"

"Good morning!" we shouted back. A boy beside me added "— teacher!" We all laughed.

"Are you the boss angel?" the same boy asked. Half of us were shocked and half laughed.

Mrs. Simms laughed. She thought about it. She nodded. "Yes, I guess you could say I'm the boss angel. But, Joseph" — she turned to the board and wrote her name in big letters — "you can call me Mrs. Simms."

Joseph nodded and looked across the aisle at me and said, "Cool." I didn't know him. I figured he must be new.

"All right," said Mrs. Simms, "let's talk about angels for a minute. You've been a baby and you've been a cat, and you know what they are. But what about angels? What's an angel?" Her eyes swept over the class. Hands went up.

"A spirit," said Raymond Venotti.

"A dead person with wings," said Holly Briscoe.

"Big *white* wings!" Jeremy Muntz called out without raising his hand.

Judy Billings was sitting in front of me. (It was no accident. I had rushed to get the seat behind

her.) Her hand shot in the air. "Ouu . . . ouu . . ."
she went.

"Yes, Judy?" said Mrs. Simms.

Judy stood even though the others didn't. "Perfect
in every way." The way she said it, so sure, I got the
impression she knew a couple of angels personally.

Mrs. Simms pointed to her. "Good. All good answers." She motioned the rest of the hands to go down. "Now, let's talk about —"

Christina Serrano practically screamed: "Mrs. Simms! Your earrings are angels!"

She was right. Dangling from Mrs. Simms's ears were little silver angels with wings.

A couple of kids clapped. A couple said, "Cool!" Beside me the new Joseph kid said, "You da chick," but not loud enough for the teacher to hear.

Mrs. Simms bowed. "Thank you, thank you, friends. You are very observant. Last year's class didn't notice till the third day of school." She clapped her hands. "All right, now, where were we —" She pointed to Judy Billings again. "Yes — perfection. I've heard that too. Whatever angels may be, everybody seems to agree that they're perfect. All right —" She looked us over. "Show of hands — anybody here perfect?"

We all turned around to see if any hands went up. One did.

Mrs. Simms seemed surprised. "Well, well, Joseph. Congratulations to you."

Joseph grinned and slapped his own hand down. "Nah. Just kidding."

Mrs. Simms pretended to wipe her brow. "Whew . . . had me worried there for a second. I wouldn't know what to do with a perfect third-grader."

"Send him to angel school!" someone piped up. Everybody laughed — Mrs. Simms hardest of all. It was only when she stared at me and gave me a thumbs-up that I suddenly realized something: *The*

one who said it was me! I
couldn't believe it. I never did
anything like that in my life. I
never speak in class unless
I raise my hand first. What
got into me? I wondered if it
had something to do with sitting next to Joseph.

"I can see I'm going to love this class," said Mrs.
Simms. "Okay, angels are perfect. *Real* angels, that
is. But we're not really *real* angels, are we? We're
third-grade angels, people-type angels — right?"

"Right!" came the calls.

"So," she went on, "the best we can do *is*" —
she waited to build up the suspense — "the best we
can do."

A couple "Huhs?" popped up.

"In other words," said Mrs. Simms, "in order to be good third-grade angels, all you have to do is *do . . . your . . . best.*" She looked us over. "Got it?"

"Got it!" we said.

"Okay," said Mrs. Simms. "But I know you guys. You like a little reward for your trouble, right?"

"Right!"

"You want a little prize at the end of the road. To make it all worthwhile — right?"

"Right!"

"Well —" she said. She reached into her desk drawer. "Have I got a prize for you —"

2

THE PRIZE

It was a circle of yellow cardboard.

"Halo!" voices called.

"Halo it is," said Mrs. Simms. "Wonder if it fits." She put it on her head. She smiled and blinked her eyes, like an angel, I guess. We laughed.

"So," she said, "who would like to win a halo?"

Every hand went up — but one. Mrs. Simms looked surprised. "Not you, Joseph?"

Joseph shrugged. He dragged his hand into the air. "Sure, why not."

She nodded. "Indeed, why not. So, here's the deal. Beginning in October, one angel per week will get to wear a puppy just like this —" By "puppy" she meant halo, which she waved at us. "When your *boss angel* week is over" — she grinned at Joseph — "you may take your halo home. You may sleep with it for all I care."

We laughed again.

"So, you ask, how do I get my halo, Mrs. Teacher?" She pointed at us. "Hah, good question. *Becoming an angel?* Foof — that was easy. All you had to do was make it to third grade. But this" — she jabbed the halo at us — "*this* . . . you have to work for. *This* . . . you have to *earn*."

Billy Umberger's hand was waving. "How do we earn it, Mrs. Simms?"

She blew Billy Umberger a kiss. "I love a kid who asks good questions." We laughed. We were spending a lot of time laughing. "Let me throw the question back to you guys." (She called us "guys." Cool.) "What do *you* think you have to do to win your halo?"

Hands went up. She called on Judy Billings. Judy had a butterfly thing holding her hair back from her right ear. I had liked Judy Billings ever since first grade, but I never before had such a good look at the back of her ear. Talk about *perfect*! Any angel would be proud to have that ear.

"Be good!" Judy said, like she was daring anybody to disagree.

"Okay —" said Mrs. Simms. She repeated it as she wrote it on the board: "BE . . . GOOD." She turned back to us. "What else? . . . Ronald?"

"Help people," said Ronald Chu.

Mrs. Simms wrote on the board: HELPFUL. She looked us over. "Jendayi?"

Jendayi Owens said, "Be nice."

NICE, wrote Mrs. Simms.

And so it went.

"Friendly!"

"Obedient!" (Mrs. Simms wrote: BEHAVE. Joseph put his hand over his mouth and whispered real low: "Boo." He looked at me and grinned.)

"Do your homework!"

"Eat your vegetables!" (That was Bernard Webber. Lots of laughing and groaning, but Mrs. Simms wrote it.)

"Wash your ears!"

"Neat cubbies!" (That was me.)

"Spelling!"

"Give the teacher an apple!" (That was Joseph. Laughing and clapping. Mrs. Simms wrote: LOVE YOUR TEACHER. Big cheers. Even a whistle.)

By the time the last hand was called on, the board was almost full. Mrs. Simms took a deep breath. "Well . . . there you go. Look how many ways there are to earn your halo. Get the picture, angels?"

"Yes!" we shouted.

She snapped her fingers and pointed to us. "All right, then. I've done my job. The rest is up to you."

She looked at the calendar on the wall. "Twenty-five days till October. I wonder which angel will be first to get a halo."

We all wondered with her.

"Mrs. Simms!" It was Billy Umberger — itching for another kiss, I figured.

"Yes, Billy?"

"Does everybody get a halo?"

Mrs. Simms blinked, like the question surprised her. "I hope so. I expect every one of you to prove to me you're worthy of being an angel. I've been doing this for twelve years now, and so far every one of my students has earned his or her halo."

Somebody blurted, "Even Gerald Willis?"

I heard gasps. Twenty-three heads jerked in my direction — because the somebody who blurted was *me*!

Joseph reached across and punched my arm. "You da dude."

I couldn't believe myself. All of a sudden it was like there was no door between my brain and my mouth. As for Gerald Willis, he was a fifth-grader, a troublemaker, and a bully.

The class was laughing, but Mrs. Simms wasn't even smiling. She stared at me. "I *said* everybody."

I wanted to jump to my feet and call out, *I'm sorry, Mrs. Simms! I don't know what's getting into me! I'm not usually a big mouth!*

The bell rang for recess.

I was first out the door.

3

BOINK, BUNK

"**B**oink."

I heard the word and felt something hit the back of my head at the same time.

I turned. It was Joseph.

"What was that?" I said.

"This," he said. He held out a pack of gummy bears. "Take one."

"Nah," I said, because I don't like gummy bears. And then, for some strange reason, I heard myself say "Okay" and I was reaching out and taking a green one. "Thanks."

"No problem." He took one — a red one — and stuffed the pack in his pocket. "So, George, what do you think of all this angel bunk?"

"It's not George," I told him. "It's Suds. George is just on my birth certificate."

"I know what you mean," he said. "I'm Joey." He sneered. "I hate Joseph. Teachers always do that."

He held out his fist. I stared at it. "Bump me, dude," he said.

"Oh," I said. I bumped him. I guess I did it right because he didn't laugh or sneer. It was my first-ever fist bump.

"So," he said again, "what do you think of all that angel bunk?"

I had heard him the first time. I didn't know what to say because, to tell the truth, I didn't think it was bunk. (I didn't recognize the word "bunk," but it sounded bad.) "Oh . . . I don't know," I said.

"Where's it all come from?" he said.

I recited the chant for him. I stopped at "Third grade angels."

He sneered. He wagged his head. "Dumb. We didn't do nothin' like that at my school."

I was thinking, *This is your school now.* But I said, "Where was that?"

He gave me a name I never heard of. And said, "So what's fourth grade?"

"Rats," I said.

His whole face changed, like he had just ripped open the best birthday present he ever got. "Whoa. Rats. *Cool.* I'm gonna like next year."

I'm not, I thought.

We were standing by the fence, near the swings.

"I saw you looking at her," he said.

"Huh?" I said, even though I knew exactly what he was talking about.

He chuckled. "Don't pretend." He poked me in the arm. "And don't look away. You were looking at her the whole time."

"Who?" I said.

"The hottie," he said, grinning. He nodded toward the girl on the swing. "What's her name?"

"Judy Billings."

"So you like her, huh?"

"Heck no," I said.

He grinned. "You were looking at her in class too. I thought you were gonna mash your nose into the back of her head."

"I was *not*," I said.

He laughed. He poked me again.

Things were getting complicated. I started to walk away. He grabbed my arm. "Hey," he said, "who's that?" He was pointing to a big kid sitting on the bottom end of the sliding board. A line of kids was waiting at the top to slide down, but nobody was telling the big kid to move.

"Gerald Willis," I said.

"The kid you were talking about in class?"

"Yeah. He's in fifth grade."

"He was a rat last year?"

"Yeah."

"Was he the boss rat?"

"Yeah, I guess so," I said.

The way Joey was looking at Gerald Willis, I could tell he wanted to be boss rat someday. Then suddenly he was running across the playground to the sliding board. He pushed his way to the top of the ladder, threw out his hands, yelled "Geronimo!" and slid down — right into the back of Gerald Willis. It was like a monkey crashing into a gorilla. Gerald Willis didn't flinch. Joey, faster than you could think, hopped with both feet onto Gerald's shoulders, pushed off, and hit the ground running. Gerald Willis was screaming bad words after him, but Joey was only laughing.

By the time he got back to me, his face was red and his eyes were flashing. He was gasping for breath. Everybody was staring, including Judy

Billings. Her swing wasn't moving. And then Joey was walking — *over to her!* He stood in front of her, still gasping, kind of hunched over. She stared at him. Her mouth was open.

He turned back to me. His red face was grinning. His arm came up. It was pointing at me. He squeezed out words between gasps: "He . . . loves . . . you."

Judy didn't move at first, like she didn't hear him. Then her head started turning real slow, till it stopped at me. Her face was still the same — boggled — like she was in the front row at a movie. The only other thing that moved was Gerald Willis, who was heading for Joey. I went into a coma, and then the school bell was ringing and kids were running for the door.

4

TUB TALK

What a day! It felt like a chipmunk was darting around inside me, trying to get out. "Chipmunky," Mom calls it.

As soon as I got home I headed straight upstairs. I turned on the bathwater and poured in Bubble Tubble. Two minutes later I was in the tub and soap bubbles were rising like snow around me. This is what I do when I need to calm down. It was Mom's idea from when I was little. It's how I got the name Suds.

My mother came in. She always seems to know when I'm in the suds. "Chipmunky?" she said.

"Yeah," I said.

She put the toilet lid down and sat. "And only the first day of school."

"I never had such a crazy first day," I told her. "Or *any* day."

She scooped a handful of suds and blew them at me. I laughed. Already the chipmunk was slowing down.

She saw my tugboat and dinosaur on the shelf. "Wow," she said. "You must've been in a big hurry. You forgot your pals. Want them?"

I nodded. She dumped them into the tub. They sank into the suds.

"So," she said, "want to tell me about it?"

I told her about it. When I'm in the suds, I tell everything.

I told her about Mrs. Simms saying "Welcome, angel George" and shaking my hand and talking to us about how we were going to be angels. I told her how we laughed a lot and that Mrs. Simms took out the halo and that we had to earn our halos and that she believed every one of us would do it and she wondered who would be the first.

"And I kept blurting out stuff," I told her. "Without even raising my hand."

She looked surprised. "Really? That doesn't sound like you. You're not a blurter."

"I *know*," I said. "But I was today." Then I told her about the new kid, Joey. "I think he's a troublemaker."

"Really?" she said. "How so?"

"Well, he whispers stuff in class and he kinda talks like an older kid and he doesn't want to be an angel." I suddenly remembered. "He called Judy Billings a hottie."

Mom didn't look impressed. "I think Mrs. Simms can handle him."

"I don't think he's afraid of Mrs. Simms," I told her. "I don't think he's afraid of *anybody*."

"Do tell?"

"You know what he did on the playground at recess?"

"I can't wait."

"He slid down the sliding board right into Gerald Willis! And then he jumped off Gerald's shoulders and ran away laughing."

"My, my."

She still didn't seem impressed. "Mom, do you *hear* what I'm saying? Gerald *Willis*."

She touched her ears and quick pulled her hands away. "My ears are burning."

I laughed. Then stopped. "But that wasn't the main thing," I said.

"So what was the main thing?"

I reached deep in the suds for my dinosaur. I took a deep breath. "Joey told Judy Billings I love her."

Mom's eyebrows went up. That was the only hint that she was impressed. Then she gave a shrug. "So? What's the big deal? You've been in love with Judy Billings since first grade."

I screamed: "Mom!"

She patted my head. "Calm down, boy. Don't scream at your mother. Did I just say something that's not true? Did I lie?"

All I could do was stare at her. She does this to me. She tricks me with words.

She laughed. "What you're trying to say is, 'Mom, that's *not* the point.'" She pressed the end of my nose with a sudsy fingertip. "Right?"

"Right," I said. "That's not the point."

"So, Kokomo, what *is* the point?"

"The point is, he *said* it. Out *loud*. To *her.*"

"And you don't want her to know it?"

"No," I said, like *Why would I?*

"But you tell her you love her in every Valentine's Day card."

Sometimes even my own mother can be dumb. "Mom — that's *Valentine's* Day."

She nodded. "Oh. Right. I forgot."

"So," I said, "you see the problem?"

She nodded. "I do."

"What's going to happen when I go to *school* tomorrow? When she *sees* me?"

She looked at me. "Well, let me ask *you* a question. What are you *afraid* is going to happen?"

I tried to think about it, but I wasn't having any luck. "I don't know," I said. "Something really bad."

"Want to hear what I predict?"

"What?"

"I predict nothing will happen."

I stared at her. "Nothing?"

"Nothing. Zero. Zip." Her face tilted. "You don't believe me?" I shrugged. She laughed. "Sudsy . . . Sudsy . . . Why are you always complaining to me about Judy Billings?"

I tried to think. "I don't know."

She pressed my nose again. "She *ignores* you. She doesn't smile at you. She doesn't say hello —"

"She does if I say hello first," I said.

"Okay, but basically she ignores you, right?"

It was true. I just didn't like hearing it from my mother. "I guess," I said.

My mother smacked her knee and stood up. "Okay, then. So, I predict" — she held up one finger — "nothing bad at all will happen. Judy Billings will not laugh at you. She will not spit on you. Nothing will change. Judy Billings will simply ignore you — like she always has."

I felt better.

"I also predict" — she held up two fingers — "you will stop chipmunking about it. And my final prediction" — three fingers — "is that you and Judy Billings and everybody else will forget about who loves who because you'll all be too busy being superstar angels." She opened the bathroom door. She sent me a thumbs-up. "Got it?"

I sent a thumbs-up back to her. "Got it."

She left. I settled deeper into Bubble Tubble. I wasn't sure if I believed all of her predictions. But I did believe one. Already the chipmunk was gone.

5

THE HAT

Mom was right.

Judy Billings didn't spit at me or say hello or look at me or anything in school today. In other words, she ignored me like every other day. Even when she dropped her pencil on the floor during Silent Reading and I picked it up and handed it to her, she didn't say thank you.

And my mother was right about the angel stuff

too. From the moment Mrs. Simms said "Good morning, angels!" and we all answered "Good morning, Mrs. Simms!" you could feel the angel buzz in the air. Darren Tapp, who never says please or thank you, raised his hand and said, "Mrs. Simms, may I *please* go to the bathroom?" And when Darren came back, Missy Haverbeck, who is the shyest person in class, whispered to him as he went past her desk, "Your fly is open."

All day long *pleases* and *thank yous* and *pardon mes* were flying around like bees at a picnic.

A lot of *who did its?* too. Because from the first minute, all eyes were on Mrs. Simms's desk. Sitting right there was an apple. A really big red apple. A really big red *polished* apple. Buffed to a shine like it was a new car.

Whispers raced up and down the aisles:

"Who did it?"

"Who did it?"

"Who did it?"

Nobody knew.

Except me.

As the whispers were flying around, I was doing my usual thing in my seat behind Judy Billings: staring at her perfect, uncovered right ear. I started to notice something. The perfect curve at the top of her ear was getting pink. Then red. The whispers were flying and Judy Billings was blushing. *Ah hah!* I thought. The apple came from *her.*

Some of Judy Billings's blush sank into my chest. We shared a secret. I closed my fist and made a vow. Nothing — *nothing* — not a hundred spiders or torture by tickling or ten Gerald Willises would ever make me rat her out.

During Silent Reading, Mrs. Simms was writing something. It was hard to concentrate on my book. I kept looking up at her. So did everybody else. We were all wondering the same thing: Is she writing something good about me?

Perfect in every way.

I kept remembering what Judy Billings said about angels yesterday. And that's what we were today — perfect in every way. We sat straight in our chairs and raised our hands for every question and stood to give our answers and were quiet as mice the rest of the time. I kept reminding myself to keep my lip buttoned and not blurt out stuff like yesterday. Only Joey was bad. He kept making

noises and funny faces. He was trying to make us laugh, but nobody did.

Even in the lunchroom we were perfect. Everybody smiled at the lunch ladies and said thank you whenever they handed us something. And everybody chewed with mouths shut. Except Joey.

Then came after-lunch recess.

It was a warm and sunny day, but really windy. Swings were flapping when nobody sat on them. Basketball shots were curving. Besides the wind, everything was going along pretty normal until a yellow baseball cap came flying onto the playground. On the other side of the fence a lady in a sweat suit was stopped, jogging in place. She was pointing to her hat, which had blown off and landed among a bunch of us third-graders.

For a second, nobody moved. And then it hit all of us at once: *Good deed!* About ten of us pounced on the hat. There were so many hands the best I could do was grab somebody's wrist. We were wrenching and pulling and twisting ten different ways.

"I got it!"

"I got it!"

"Let go!"

"I was first!"

"I was first!"

"Oww!"

Suddenly we all snapped apart like a broken wishbone. Eddie Shank was holding the rim of the cap. Diana Briggs was holding the rest.

Somebody said, "Uh-oh."

Everybody just stared at the hat pieces. Except Joey, who was laughing.

A screech came from the sidewalk: "You little hoodlums!"

The jogger lady kicked the chain-link fence and started running.

Mrs. Simms was standing in the doorway, watching.

*   *   *

Silence in the classroom. The two pieces of the yellow hat sat on Mrs. Simms's desk. In between them was the apple.

"*That* was disgraceful," said Mrs. Simms. "Very un-angelic behavior."

Judy Billings raised her hand. Mrs. Simms didn't call on her, but Judy stood up and spoke anyway. "But *I* didn't do it. I was just watching." It sounded like she might cry.

Mrs. Simms didn't even look Judy's way. Judy sat down.

"You're *all* guilty," said Mrs. Simms. "You're guilty of doing it. You're guilty of watching and doing nothing to stop it. How many of you went over to the lady and told her you were sorry for the bad behavior of your classmates?" No hands. "Didn't think so. You're guilty of that too."

She looked at us like we were burnt toast. "Angels? Hah! This may be the first class where *nobody* gets a halo. Angels? You were no better than a pack of sharks after a piece of meat."

Joey burst out laughing.

"Button it, Peterson," said Mrs. Simms.

Joey buttoned it. The rest of us stopped breathing.

"I guess it was all just words, huh?" said Mrs. Simms. "Angel talk. No angel do. *This*" — she held up half a hat in each hand — "will *never* happen again." Her eyes went up and down the rows, zapping each of us with a *yeah, you* glare. She put the hat-halves down. "Got it?"

No sounds came from us. We just boggled and nodded.

6

IT WAS TRUE

"It was amazing," I said at dinner.

"You're just having one amazing day after another," said Mom.

"What was amazing?" said Zippernose. Zippernose is my sister. She's behind me, in second grade. Other people call her Amy. She sneaked a pickle chip into my peanut-butter-and-jelly sandwich on Saturday, so I'm not talking to her this week.

"Okay," said my dad, "*I'll* ask. What was so amazing?"

"Lots of stuff," I said. "A lady's hat blew onto the playground and we went after it like sharks after a piece of meat."

"You're a piece of meat!" said Zippernose.

"Mom!" I yelled.

Bubba, my baby brother, laughed and babbled something. It's the weirdest thing — whenever I get mad, he laughs. My parents understand his babble but I don't.

"We?" said my dad.

"Huh?" I said.

"You said '*we* went after it like sharks.' You were one of the sharks?"

"I'm a cat," said Zippernose. She hates it when I get all the attention.

"I guess I was," I said. "But it wasn't me that ripped the hat apart."

My mother's eyes boggled. "Ripped it *apart*? Good grief. What did the lady say?"

"She called us little hoodlums."

"She got *that* right."

"And Mrs. Simms saw it all."

"Good."

"But *I* didn't rip it," I told them. "There were too many hands in there. I couldn't even feel the hat."

"Accessory to the crime," said Dad. "You were all equally guilty." My dad's a lawyer.

I stabbed a green bean. "That's what Mrs. Simms said. Even the kids who were just watching were guilty."

Dad nodded. "I like this teacher."

"I'm a cat," said Zippernose. I saw her reaching

for the mashed-potato spoon. I got there first. I dumped a spoonful on my plate. She reached for the spoon. I put it on the other side of the table. She screeched bloody murder. "Mom! He always has to be first! He saw me reaching for the spoon and grabbed it!"

"Give her the spoon," said Dad.

Zippernose's hand was wagging in my face. I stuck the spoon in the mashed potatoes.

She went on whining. "He just did it to make me mad. He doesn't even *like* mashed potatoes."

I ignored her. "Mrs. Simms was really mad," I said. "She told us we were disgraceful. She said maybe nobody will get a halo this year. And you know what she said to Joey Peterson?"

"The new kid who's not afraid of anybody?" said Mom.

"Yeah. Him. He laughed when she called us sharks and know what she said?"

"What?" said Zippernose.

I didn't answer.

"What?" said Dad.

"She said 'Button it, Peterson.'"

Dad grinned. "I like this teacher."

As I said before, I do a lot of talking in the tub (to my mom). As for thinking, I do that in bed. And that's what I was doing, thinking about dinner and hearing Zippernose's words over and over: *He always has to be first.*

It really bugged me because it's bad enough I have to hear her voice all day long in the house. But now I was hearing it in my own dark and private bed with the door shut and the lights out. It was like she

shrunk herself and crawled into my ear and now she was holding a megaphone and shouting across my brain: *He always has to be first . . . He always has to be first . . .*

There was another reason why it bugged me.

She was right.

I could never say it to anybody. I couldn't even say it to my mother from under the suds in the tub. In fact, until this night, I don't think I had ever said it to *myself.*

But as soon as she said it at the dinner table, I knew it was true. And it was about everything, not just mashed-potato spoons.

When us kids have races, I almost always win. If I don't, I feel bad. I mean, *really* bad.

When we do art or writing in school, I'm always the neatest. The other kids come to my desk to see my stuff. My lines are straight. My letters are perfect. Even in first grade, I never colored outside the lines. Last year my teacher said, "George, you may be the neatest student I've ever had."

I almost never spell a word wrong. If I do, it bugs me for days.

If I'm in the hallway heading for the bathroom and I see Zippernose coming from the other direction, I run to get there first. I can't help it. It's like *everything* is a race that I have to win.

And now that's how I feel about getting a halo.

I want to be first.

I *have* to be first.

7

"DON'T BUY ME"

Eleven!

That's how many apples were lined up along the front of Mrs. Simms's desk. Plus two pears, a banana, and a sandwich. And that's not counting Judy Billings's apple from yesterday, which Mrs. Simms took home last night. And one other thing: a gummy bear, a red one (from guess who).

One of the apples was from me.

We sat in our seats staring at them. Mrs. Simms

stared. We were remembering how mad she was when school ended yesterday. We were all flinching . . . waiting . . .

And then it came. It started with a little wrinkle at her mouth. Then it went to her eyes. Then her whole face. Her cheeks bulged out like tennis balls.

Her neck got ropey. Her hand shot to her mouth. *Omygod*, I thought, *she's gonna barf!* I inched back in my seat. Sure enough, something exploded from her, but it wasn't barf. Whatever it was, it wasn't just a mouth thing. It was a full-body thing. She bent over like she had a stomachache. She twirled away from us and wobbled to the front wall and stopped herself with her hand before crashing into it. When she turned back to us and took her hand away, I didn't recognize her face. It was blotchy and lumpy and red. Tears were coming down her cheeks. It was scary.

Somebody peeped, "Is she crying?"

Somebody else peeped, "She's sick."

Joey Peterson gave a snort. "She ain't crying, dummy. She ain't sick. She's laughing."

He was right! She *was* laughing. I never knew a teacher could laugh so hard.

Joey was chuckling to himself. The rest of us were a fishbowl of open mouths.

Finally she started to calm down. She took deep breaths.

I looked around. A couple kids were smiling. So I did too. But I was still afraid to laugh out loud. I had a feeling this might be a trick.

She pulled a tissue from her box of Kleenex. She wiped her eyes and cheeks. She took a long, deep breath. She picked up the sandwich. It was plastic-wrapped. She stared at it. She held it out to us. "Okay . . ." she said, "what is it?"

Billy Umberger spoke. "Corned beef."

Mrs. Simms nodded. "Hmmm."

It looked like she was ready to bust out again, but she took a deep breath. She sniffed. "O-*kay*. Students. This has never happened before. I guess

I wasn't ready for it. Sorry for losing my self-control there. Disgraceful example for my students."

"That's okay, Mrs. Simms."

She turned to me and smiled — *because I was the one who said it.* I kicked myself in the ankle. "Thank you, George," she said.

"Go Georgie," I heard Joey whisper.

"I want you to know —" said Mrs. Simms. She put down the corned-beef sandwich and stepped away from the desk, so we could all see the lineup again. "I want you to know how much I appreciate all this." She waved at it but she still couldn't look at it. "But I have to make something clear to you. *Very* clear. Yes — you must earn your halo. But no — you may not *buy* your halo. I can*not* be bribed." She looked us over. "Can somebody tell me what a bribe is?"

One hand went up: Ian O'Hara's.

"Yes, Ian?"

"It means when you pay money to somebody to make them do something you want."

Mrs. Simms nodded. "Yes. Good, Ian. With one correction. A bribe doesn't have to be money. A bribe can be" — she waved at the desk — "apples. Or pears. Or bananas. Or corned-beef sandwiches."

A couple kids laughed at that. "Or" — she picked up the candy — "gummy bears." She studied it for a minute, then popped it into her mouth. Everybody laughed.

Joey fist-pumped. "Yes!"

"You can bring me an apple every day. You can bring me a banana split with cherries and hot fudge and whipped cream up to the ceiling. You can bring me" — she threw out her arms — "a new car!" We laughed. "But" — her voice got lower, slower — "you . . . can*not* . . . bribe . . . your way . . . to . . . a . . . halo." She gave us her waiting-to-sink-in look. "So . . . *how* do you get your halo?"

The class called back: "Earn it!"

"Lesson learned, student angels?"

"Yes!"

"Okay. So. Stop putting your energy into bribes. Put your energy into being good. Into *doing* good. Impress me. Don't buy me." She rooted in a desk drawer and came out with a plastic bag. She dumped in the pears and the banana. She sniffed the sandwich. "Corned beef, huh? Mr. Moto will like this." Mr. Moto is her dog. Into the bag went the sandwich.

Mrs. Simms got another plastic bag and dropped in the apples. "These," she said, "will become my famous pink applesauce."

8

PERFECT

For our first work of the day, we started to learn cursive. The twenty-six letters — capitals and little ones — were written on a green track across the top of the board. Our job was to copy the capitals, *A* to *Z*. Five times each.

I was super neat and careful. I kept the letters perfectly between the blue lines on the paper — except when they had to go below for the *J*, *Y*, and *Z*. Mrs. Simms walked around, looking over our shoulders. When she stopped next to me, she tapped her finger on my desk and whispered, "Good."

We did map reading. Mrs. Simms spun the big globe. She asked who could come up and point to the Indian Ocean. She called on Noah Jablonski. He missed it. She called on Diana Briggs. Not even close. She called on me. I nailed it!

In math, Mrs. Simms said by the end of the year we're going to add and subtract numbers up to — she wrote it on the board — 10,000. "How much is that?" she said.

Joey called out, "A million!"

Mrs. Simms didn't even look at him. When you don't raise your hand, she ignores you.

I raised my hand. She called on me. "Ten thousand," I said. I was right.

Mrs. Simms read us a story. It was about a city kid who spends his summer on a farm. When she came to a strange word, she stopped. The word was "husbandry."

"Anybody know what 'husbandry' means?" she asked the class.

Only one hand went up. Emma Feldman said, "A married man."

Wrong.

Joey's hand shot up. "*Two* married men!"

Everybody laughed.

I raised my hand.

"George?"

"Could I go to the dictionary and look it up?"

She smiled. "Be my guest."

I went to the dictionary. It sits on its own little table, called a podium. Mrs. Simms spelled the word for me. I looked it up. I read aloud: "On a farm, growing crops and raising animals."

A couple kids clapped. Joey whistled. Mrs. Simms glared at him, but I could tell she wasn't really mad.

In the playground I did a nice thing. We chose sides for a basketball game. I was a chooser. I chose the best players — until the last one. Then I chose Walter Glipner. Everyone was shocked,

including Walter. Nobody ever chooses Walter. When he shoots the ball, forget about the basket — he can't even hit the *backboard*! When Walter got over the shock, he stuffed his glasses in his pocket and cried out, "Let's go!"

I never saw a kid so happy and excited. It made me feel good. Mrs. Simms was at the fence talking to another teacher. I wondered if she saw what I did.

At lunch we had sloppy joes. And a green vegetable. Peas. Three days a week we have a green vegetable. I never take it. This time I did.

I was the only one at my table with peas. Joey picked one out of my dish and flicked it at Bernard Webber. Secretly I hoped the other guys would dig in and start a big pea fight until there weren't any peas left. I ate my sloppy joe as slow as I could. I drank my chocolate milk. And still my dish was full

 of peas, minus one. Lunch hour was almost over. I gobbled them down. I tried not to taste.

But on the way back to class I felt good. I felt like an angel.

That's how I felt for the rest of the day. As I walked out of the classroom I said, "Good-bye, Mrs. Simms."

She said, "Good-bye, George." And the way she smiled at me — it was like she was sending me a message: *You were perfect today.*

I was first onto the bus. As I sat there, I replayed the day in my head. Mrs. Simms was right — I *was* perfect!

I sat up straight in my bus seat. I looked out. I saw Mrs. Simms standing at our classroom window.

I'm pretty sure she was looking at me. I'm pretty sure she was smiling.

In a couple minutes, the bus was mobbed. Zippernose flopped into a seat right across the aisle from me. She had to lean forward because her pink backpack was so stuffed. She didn't look at me. She was gabbing away with some other second-grader in the seat in front of her. It was the weirdest feeling when I realized I was looking at her. I never look at her. But I was.

And that's when a really scary question came to me.

9

SPIES

"Does it count if the teacher doesn't see it?"

My mother was in the backyard. She was cutting stuff from her herb garden. Her head came up. "Say again?"

"If Mrs. Simms doesn't see me being good, how am I supposed to get credit for my halo?"

She snipped a couple stems and stood up. She turned around. I laughed. She was wearing the

supersize movie-star sunglasses I gave her as a joke for her birthday. "In other words," she said, "you want to know if it's okay to be bad when you're not at school."

Another word trick. I was thinking it over when Zippernose came screeching. "Mommy! Mommy! Let me wear them!" She was jumping up, grabbing for the glasses.

I smacked her hand away. "No."

She punched me. (Her punches don't hurt.) "*You* shut up. They're Mommy's glasses."

"*I* gave them to her," I said.

"Which makes them *mine*," said my mother. She took them off and handed them to Zippernose. "One minute and give them back."

Zippernose went dancing across the yard.

I heard a chuckle. My mother was grinning down

at me. "So," she said, "what you *really* want to know is if you *have* to be nice to your sister — right?"

My mother is unbeliev-able. She not only knows the answers, she knows the *questions*.

"Well . . ." I said, ". . . sorta."

She nodded. The grin was gone. A serious answer was coming. "Okay, here's what I think. You like Mrs. Simms, right?"

"Yes," I said.

"You like her because she's nice, right?"

"Right."

"And nice people usually have a lot of friends, wouldn't you say?"

"I guess so."

"So" — she sniffed her handful of herbs — "Mrs. Simms — nice Mrs. Simms — probably has a lot of friends. You with me?"

It's funny. My dad is the lawyer, but my mom often sounds like one. "Yeah," I said.

"So here's what I think." She jabbed the herbs at me. "I think it's not just Mrs. Simms keeping an eye on you. I think it's her network of friends too. They're probably all over the place. If they see one of her students acting up, they report back to her."

"You mean, like spies?" I said.

She nodded. "Sort of." She brushed the herbs across my nose. I smelled mint. "If you ask my advice, I'd say you better not take a chance. You better be nice to everybody *all* the time. And that" — she poked the herbs at the dancing Zippernose — "sad

to say, ol' Sudsie, includes your dear little sister."
She called, "Amy, time's up!"

Zippernose squealed. "One more minute!"

Mom held out her hand. "Now." She said it in her
don't mess with me voice.

Zippernose groaned and slugged over and gave
up the glasses. She gave me her best *I hate you* face
and said "Poop" and punched me, like it was all my

fault. Usually I would hit her back. Instead I looked at the neighbors' backyards. At the neighbors' windows. I wondered if a spy was lurking behind a shade. I let Zippernose go grumping off un-hit. And then Mom was squeezing me and saying, "My little angel."

10

ANGEL AT HOME

It's harder to be an angel at home than at school.

I mean, it's not like I'm *really* bad at home. I don't throw the remote. I don't make fires in the living room. I don't say bad words. I'm just a normal kid. I do *normal* bad things. Sometimes I whine if I don't get my way. Or leave my underwear on the floor. Or forget to cap the toothpaste or turn out lights. Or stick a banana peel under Zippernose's pillow.

But you should see me now. I sit up straight at

the dinner table. I don't pick at my food. When I answer the phone I say, "Morton residence. May I help you?" Every piece of dirty clothes goes into the hamper. If I need the salt, I say, "Salt, please." When somebody passes it, I say, "Thank you." I don't have to worry about thanking my sister, because she would never pass me anything. But I don't call her Zippernose anymore (except in my head). I don't call her Amy either. I don't call her anything.

Now that I think about it, the only really hard thing about being an angel at home is being nice to my sister. And even that seemed pretty easy until my mother had a little talk with me a week ago.

"So," she said, "how's the halo hunt going?"

"Okay," I said.

"How many more days till the crowning of the first perfect angel?"

She knew I was counting. "Eighteen," I said.

She whistled. "Eighteen more days. No lights on in empty rooms. No clothes on the floor. This is a new experience for me — a perfect person right here" — she pointed straight down — "in *my* house."

"Thanks," I said.

"Or maybe I should say *almost* perfect."

"Huh?" I said.

"Well, there is one little area where . . . well . . . you're not exactly bad, but you're not exactly good either. You're just kind of nothing."

"I am?"

"Yes. With your sister. I thought we agreed you're going to be nice to her."

I couldn't believe she was saying this. "Mom, I *am* nice to her. I didn't hit her for a *week*. I don't make fun of her. I don't slam the door on

her face. Mom — I don't even call her Zippernose anymore."

She nodded. "True. You don't *do* anything. And that's" — she poked me — "the point, joint. You ignore her. Like Judy Billings ignores you. It's as if she doesn't exist. That's not being nice to her. Being nice means doing *something*, not doing *nothing*." She held out her fist. "Dig it?"

I nodded. "Dig it." We fist-bumped.

So for the past week I've been doing one nice thing for my sister each day. Like, yesterday at breakfast, after I used the pancake syrup, instead of keeping it on my side of the table, I pushed it back to the middle where she could reach it. And today, when I saw her Plumpy Donkey on the hallway floor — usually I would step on it. But not this time.

 This time I just kicked it back into her room.

So far it's not so bad. Because every time I do something nice, I think: *Maybe one of Mrs. Simms's spies saw that.* I keep sneaking looks at the windows, but so far I haven't caught anybody peeking in. I can almost feel them. Spying. Taking notes. (Maybe even pictures!) Reporting back to Mrs. Simms. I have to really be on my toes. I have to make up for all that blurting. I can't lose focus.

Good. Good. Good.

Nice. Nice. Nice.

Perfect in every way.

Eleven days till October first. Eleven days till First Halo.

11

THE RACE

I feel myself getting perfecter and perfecter. Every night I go to bed thinking I can't get any better. And the next day I find out I can.

Like, one morning after I pushed through the door at school, I noticed that Constantina Pappas was behind me. Until then, the only girl I had ever held a door for was Judy Billings. Now, whenever there's a girl behind me, no matter who it is, I hold the door for her.

I pick up litter. At first I picked up stuff I stepped on in the playground. I  put it in my pocket and dumped it in a trash can in school. Then I started walking halfway across the playground to pick up candy wrappers. A couple times I caught Mrs. Simms looking my way. Now I pick up stuff from our sidewalk and gutter at home and even at the mall. Every time I do it I picture one of Mrs. Simms's spies making another check mark after my name:

MORTON ✓✓✓✓✓

In school I got all my two- and three-times tables right. And when Mrs. Simms wrote

$$100,841$$

on the board, I was the only one with the right answer: "One hundred thousand eight hundred and forty-one." And during cursive practice one day,

Mrs. Simms whispered to me: "You write better than I do."

But even with all this good stuff going on, I couldn't relax. Because I didn't know how I was doing compared to everybody else. There were twenty-three other kids in my class. I figured every one of them wanted that first halo — well, except Joey Peterson. Maybe others got all their times tables right too. Maybe I wasn't the only one Mrs. Simms whispered to. Maybe if I picked up five pieces of litter one day, somebody else picked up six.

It was like I was in a race, but I couldn't see any of the other runners.

And then all of a sudden I could see them. Because of something that happened on the playground.

12

BACK TO BAD

Raymond Venotti spit.

It happened after lunch. At the swings. Raymond walked over to an empty swing, coughed up a big lunger into his mouth, and dumped it right there on the middle of the swing seat. *Wow*, I thought, *that's some litter I'm not picking up!* I looked across the way. Mrs. Simms was staring and glaring. She saw the whole thing.

I said to Raymond, "Why'd you do it?"

He shrugged. "I don't know."

"Mrs. Simms saw you," I told him.

He shrugged some more. "So?"

I was shocked. "*So? What about the halo? Don't you care?*"

He shook his head. "Nah. I'm tired of being good."

Three things happened after that:

1. A second-grade girl sat on the swing.
   After a minute she stood up. Her hand
   felt her butt. She screamed.
2. Mrs. Simms had a private talk with
   Raymond Venotti in the hallway.
3. I suddenly started seeing other stuff.

Everywhere I looked, kids were being bad. And
messy. And rude.

When Mrs. Simms had her back turned, Wilson
Banner burped out loud — on purpose.

Dawn Olichek pulled a booger from her nose and
stuck it under her seat.

Four kids had untied shoelaces.

Even Judy Billings — she dropped a gum wrapper on the ground!

I told my mother all this after school.

"Sounds like you got a bunch of regular hoodlums in there," she said.

"What's it all mean, Mom?" I asked her. "Don't they even care about the halo anymore?"

She tugged my earlobe. "What it means, Sudser, is they're just being normal third-graders. Maybe it means that *you*" — she tugged both ears — "are the *only* one trying to be a perfect angel."

I think she was telling me I didn't have to worry anymore about winning the race — because everybody else dropped out. I was the only one left.

Yes! I thought. *The halo is mine!*

But my mother was wrong.

13

CHIPMUNKY

Darren Tapp is still in the race.

I sneaked a peek at his cursive. It's as perfect as mine. And I think I saw Mrs. Simms whispering to him.

I saw him holding a door for a girl.

He sits up perfectly straight in class.

I tested him at recess. I stood next to him and dropped a piece of paper on the ground (when I was sure Mrs. Simms wasn't looking). He picked it up!

There's only one thing all this can mean: Darren Tapp wants that first halo too. I guess the big question is: Does he want it as bad as I do?

I can feel his breath on my neck.

I'm running faster and faster.

I volunteered to do the dishes at home. My father thought I was joking. He laughed. "We have a dishwasher!"

I tried to buy a box of dog biscuits with my allowance at the supermarket. "What's that for?" my mother asked.

"For Mrs. Simms's dog," I told her. "Mr. Moto."

"I thought you told me Mrs. Simms cannot be bribed," she said.

"She can't," I said. "But this isn't for her. It's for her dog."

"Put it back," she said.

Some people don't make it easy being perfect. But I'm not giving up.

When I see students heading for the water fountain, I rush ahead and push the button for them.

I hold the door for *boys*.

I don't even *think* the word "Zippernose" anymore.

It's not easy. As soon as I think I'm finally perfect, I think of something I missed.

And then there's another problem: People keep messing me up.

Like the other day in school. I was doing cursive letter *P*. Then I had to go to the bathroom. When I came back, I found a whole line of letters with an extra curl at the bottom so they looked like *B*s. I looked over at Joey. He was doing his letters, but

his face was getting red and blue from trying not to laugh. It took me five minutes just to erase the messed-up line.

That same day after school I couldn't find my teddy bear, Winky. It's always sitting up against my pillow. I finally found it in my underwear drawer. Every day I find something else where

it's not supposed to
be. I know Zip —
excuse me — *my sister*
is doing it. But until I
get my halo, I'm afraid
to fight back. So I
headed for the tub.

Mom found me in the suds.

"Oh no —" she went. "Chipmunky again?"

She was right. I've been in the tub almost every day lately.

"I'm a nervous wreck," I told her.

I don't know why that was funny, but she laughed. "Yes, I can see that." She sat on the edge of the tub. "Don't you think maybe you're getting a little carried away? Maybe you're taking this angel business a little too far?"

"I have to stay ahead of Darren Tapp," I said. "He's just waiting for me to make a mistake."

She reached into the tub and tugged my earlobe with soapy fingers. "Suds, by the end of the year everybody will have a halo. It's okay to not be first. It's okay to be second. Or tenth. Or even last."

It's okay to not be first.

I tried to wrap my brain around those words. I couldn't.

And then, yesterday, four things happened.

14

OH NO!

The First Thing happened in the morning. At recess.

I saw a candy wrapper on the ground and picked it up. Joey poked me. "Why do you keep doing that?"

"I told you before," I said. "I want the first halo."

"But look —" he said. He pointed at the school and all around the playground. "Mrs. Simms isn't even here. You're not even getting credit for it."

I grinned. "Yes I am."

He blinked. "You are?"

I got closer. I whispered, "She has spies."

He boggled. *"What?"*

"Mrs. Simms can't be watching everywhere all the time. So she has spies. Her friends."

His eyes darted around. "How do you know?"

"My mom said."

The boggle went away. He did more blinking. Then he was grinning. I mean, not just any grin. The grin was so big it was almost scary.

"What's so funny?" I said.

"Your mom," he said.

"What do you mean?"

He poked me. "She was joking you, dude. There ain't no spies."

"You calling my mom a liar?"

"I'm calling your mom a joker." He tossed a gummy bear at me. It bonked off my nose. "There ain't no spies."

There ain't no spies?

Now it was my turn to boggle.

The Second Thing happened in the afternoon.

We were riding home on the bus. My sister sat behind me. She kept taking off her seat belt and reaching over my seat and sticking her finger in my ear. She knows I can't stand that. It was getting harder and harder for me not to strike back.

So I got off the bus early.

"Hey!" she called. "It's not our stop!"

I kept walking. I prayed she wouldn't follow me. She didn't.

Two other kids got off with me. Heather Furst and Constantina Pappas.

Heather said, "This isn't your stop."

"I know," I said. I started walking for home.

I heard a scream: "Buster! Buster!"

A little black-and-white dog came around the corner. It had a leash, but there was no person on the other end of the leash. Then the person — a teenage girl — came around the corner, chasing the dog and yelling, "Buster! Buster!"

The dog was heading straight for me. It was almost close enough for me to grab the leash when it turned and started across the street. I went after it. I dove after the leash. I grabbed it. I felt the tug of the dog on the other end. I heard screaming. The teenage girl. But something else screaming too. Even louder. Brakes. I was lying in the street. I looked up. The dog at the end of the leash was inches from the front fender of a car.

Suddenly the girl was picking me up along with the dog and wrapping us in hugs and tears and a lady was coming out of the car saying, "Oh my God! Oh my God!"

I can't even remember walking the rest of the way home. What I remember is the Third Thing.

*   *   *

The Third Thing happened in my room. On my bed. I was still shaking too hard to make it to the tub. I closed my eyes. I took deep breaths. I finally started to calm down. When my brain started to work again, this is the first thought it sent to me: *Hey man, you just did the best good deed ever! Slam dunk! The halo is yours!*

Then my brain sent me Joey's words: *There ain't no spies.*

What if he was right? What if there were no spies reporting back to Mrs. Simms? What if I wasn't going to get credit? What if The Best Good Deed Ever was going to go to waste?

The Fourth Thing started with my brain talking to itself:

So don't let it go to waste.

How do I do that?

Make your own report.

So that's what I did. With my best cursive, I wrote down what happened with the dog. I included everything. "Buster! Buster!" The brakes screeching. "Oh my God! Oh my God!"

I filled up the page. I folded it real neat. I put it in an envelope. I sealed the envelope. I put the envelope in my backpack.

When I got to school today, I put the envelope on Mrs. Simms's desk. And I couldn't believe what I saw. Another envelope was already sitting there!

Oh no! I thought. *Darren Tapp must have done a slam-dunk good deed too. And wrote a report. And beat me to it!*

I was shell-shocked. I didn't raise my hand in class all day. I was more zombie than human by the time Mrs. Simms said, "Well, angels, tomorrow's the big day. One of you will be the first to get a halo."

15

THE WINNER

"Suds . . . Suds . . ."

I heard a voice calling me. A far, far away voice.

"Suds . . . Suds . . ."

Suddenly the voice was shocking, like a smashed window: "SUDS!" I was being yanked out of warm darkness. I was sitting on the edge of my bed. My mother was yelling at me. "What are you *doing*? Why aren't you ready for *school*? Your bus is coming in five *minutes*."

"I'm not going," I said. I crawled back under the blanket.

"Are you sick?" I heard her say. She put her hand on my forehead.

"No," I said. I burrowed into the pillow.

She yanked the cover off. "Then get ready for school."

"No."

"No?" She said it again, like she couldn't figure out what the word meant: *"No?* Pray tell why not?"

"I lost."

"What?"

"It's halo day. I lost. I'm not going in."

"How do you know you lost? Your teacher hasn't even announced the winner yet."

"I just know. Darren Tapp won. He's better than me. I'm not going in."

What happened next was pretty embarrassing. My mother grabbed my clothes, including my underwear, dumped them on my head, and said, "You have sixty seconds to get dressed."

I never made it to the bus. My mother had to drive me.

When I walked into class, everyone looked up. A roomful of eyes staring at me. Mrs. Simms smiled. "Welcome, George," she said. "You're just in time." She was holding the first halo.

I took my seat — and got the shock of my life. Judy Billings turned around and smiled at me and whispered, "You're gonna win."

I had a flash fantasy. I heard Mrs. Simms call my name. I saw Judy Billings put the halo on my head like a crown. Then she gave me that 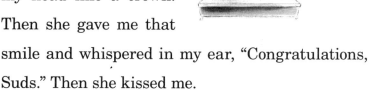 smile and whispered in my ear, "Congratulations, Suds." Then she kissed me.

But then I heard my mother's voice from the ride

in to school: "If you lose, be a good loser. It's easy to be a good winner. Any old slob can do that."

I knew the fantasy would not come true. I knew the winner would not be me.

I was right.

I knew the winner would be Darren Tapp.

I was wrong.

"Ladies and gentlemen," said Mrs. Simms in her special this-is-a-big-deal voice, "the first halo of the year goes to . . . Constantina Pappas!"

16

OUTSIDE, INSIDE

"I think I was a bad loser."

I was talking to my mother after school. I wasn't in the tub, because I wasn't stressed out. All the nervousness was gone. I felt limp as a noodle.

"How so?" said my mom. "Didn't you congratulate Constantina?"

"Yeah, I did," I told her. "When Mrs. Simms said her name, I clapped with everybody else. And when

Mrs. Simms put the halo on her head I clapped again."

"Sounds to me like you did pretty good," said my mother.

"But then something even worse happened."

"What was that?"

"In the playground. After lunch. Kids were going up and saying 'Way to go, Constantina' and stuff like that —"

I was watching the tree in our backyard. One leaf was orange and red. Fall is coming.

"And?" said my mother.

"— and then Constantina was coming toward me. She had a funny look on her face."

"Funny how?"

"I don't know," I said. "Kind of like she did something wrong. And then she took off her halo and

she said, 'I think there was a mistake. I think this is yours.' And she held out the halo to me and . . . I took it . . . and . . . and . . ."

I was crying.

Mom pulled me close to her. "Tell me."

I looked at the red leaf. I took a deep breath. "I couldn't help it, Mom. I shouldn't have took it, but

I did. I worked so hard for it. I believed her. It *was* a mistake. It really *was* mine."

I looked up. I think my mother was looking at the red leaf too. Finally she said, "And then?"

"And then — I don't know, I looked at Constantina's face and for some reason I just gave the halo back to her and walked away. I might have said 'Congratulations, Constantina,' but I'm not sure."

She pulled my ear. "You gave it back to her. Sounds to me like you're a *good* loser."

"But that's *outside*, Mom. Inside I feel like a really bad loser. Maybe the baddest loser there ever was."

"Because?"

"Because I *wanted* to keep it. I *wanted* to put it on my head and everybody would come up to *me* and say 'Congratulations, Suds.' Mom — *I was only good on the outside!*"

I was crying again.

Now both of my mother's arms were around me. That's when we heard the doorbell ring. I opened the door.

It was Mrs. Simms.

17

SURPRISE

I almost fell over.

"Hi, Mrs. Morton," she said, a big smile on her face. "Hi, Suds."

I almost fell over again. "You called me Suds."

She laughed. "Well, I'm in your territory now. So Suds it is."

My mother invited her in. We sat in the living room. My mom offered her tea or coffee or juice, but she said no thank you. The smile didn't go away,

but it changed. She took a deep breath. She spoke to my mother. "I felt I should stop by because" — now she spoke to me — "I could see how the events of the day were affecting Suds."

What was she talking about?

"Did your son tell you that the first halo went to Constantina Pappas?" she said.

"Yes, he did," said my mother, "as soon as he got home from school."

Mrs. Simms reached over and gave me a knee-pat, as if I did something great. "Good," she said. "And I was happy to see you joined the others in congratulating Constantina. I know how badly you wanted that halo, Suds. I know how hard you tried."

I didn't know what to say. And I still didn't know what she was doing in my house.

Now she was looking at me like I was the only person in the world. "Suds, you *are* an angel. You'll get your halo soon enough." I got the feeling she could see inside me. "You were disappointed you didn't get it this morning, weren't you?"

"A little," I said.

"But not really surprised?"

"Not really."

"Why not?"

"I thought Darren Tapp would get it."

"Ah. Darren Tapp. Yes." She looked at my mother. "Another boss angel."

"And the blurts," I said.

Her eyes went wide. "The blurts?"

"The first couple days of school," I said. "I kept blurting out stuff without raising my hand. I guess that sunk me."

Mrs. Simms and my mother both broke out laughing. I don't know what was so funny.

When Mrs. Simms stopped laughing, she said, "So you must have been *really* surprised that Constantina Pappas got it."

I nodded.

"Because you didn't even think she was very interested, did you? You didn't think she was even trying." She poked my knee. "Did you?"

"No," I said.

"Well, guess what?" she said.

"What?"

"You were right. She had no interest in getting the halo. Not at all. She wasn't even trying."

"Really?" I said. This was getting more and more confusing.

She nodded. "Really. And then a funny thing happened. In all my years of doing angel halos, it's never happened before." She stopped talking and just stared at me.

After a while, it occurred to me that I was supposed to ask what happened. So I did. "What happened?"

"Remember the day you put the note on my desk? Telling me how you saved the runaway dog in the street?"

"Yes."

"Well, somebody else left a note on my desk."

"I know," I said. "Darren Tapp."

She stared at me, at my mother. She blinked. She shook her head. "No . . . not Darren Tapp. The note was from Constantina Pappas."

I just stared at her.

She leaned in toward me. "Would you like to know what Constantina's note said?"

"Okay."

"Her note told me the same thing yours did."

I was more confused than ever. "Huh?" I said.

"She told me she was up the street that day and she saw the whole thing. She saw how you ran into the street and stopped the little dog from being hit by the car. She said it was such a wonderful thing you did that she thought I ought to know. She wanted me to know that you were an angel even after school."

"Oh oh oh," I heard my mother say. I looked at her. Her eyes were glittery.

"And that's why I gave the first halo to Constantina Pappas," said Mrs. Simms. "Because — yes — she *was* trying to get the halo, not for herself, but" — she smiled — "*for somebody else.*"

My mom gave a little whistle. She was fanning her face with her hand.

Mrs. Simms stood up. "Well, gotta go. Speaking of dogs, it's way past Mr. Moto's dinnertime."

At the door, Mrs. Simms turned and gave my mother a hug. Then she hugged me!

The door was shut when suddenly I thought of something. I pulled open the door. She was almost to the sidewalk. I called: "Mrs. Simms! My mom says you have spies! Joey Peterson says no! Who's right?"

Behind me my mother was laughing so hard I thought she might get sick. So was Mrs. Simms. She was wobbling. She hardly made it to her car.

I never got an answer.

ACKNOWLEDGMENTS

Halos to my three manuscript angels: my editor, Arthur Levine; my copyeditor, Starr Baer; and my wife, Eileen.

Follow Suds to Fourth Grade in . . .

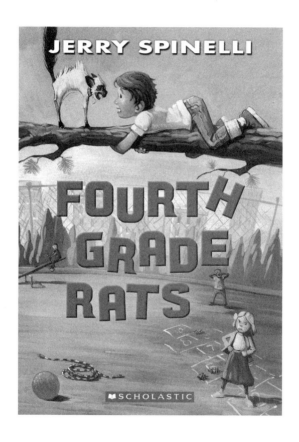

1

RATS DON'T

"First grade babies!
Second grade cats!
Third grade angels!
Fourth grade . . . RRRRRATS!"

It was the first recess of the first day of school. A mob of third-graders had me and Joey Peterson backed up against the monkey bars.

They were giving us the old chant. When they came to the word "rats," they screamed it in our faces. Then they ran off laughing.

"I wish I was still in third grade," I said.

"Why?" said Joey.

"So I could still be an angel."

"Not me." He climbed onto the first bar. "I waited three years to be a rat." He climbed to the next bar. "And now I *am* a rat."

He climbed to the top bar. He shouted over the school yard: "And proud of it!"

I started to climb. My sneaker slipped on a bar, and I went down instead of up. The first thing I landed on was my hand. My thumb got bent back, way back.

Pain!

I howled. As loud as I could.

It still hurt.

I kicked the ground, the monkey bars, the nearest tree. My thumb still hurt, and so did my foot.

Only one thing left to do. I cried.

Joey's voice came down from the high monkey bar: "Rats don't cry."

The bell rang to end recess.

I jogged, sniffling, to the door. When I got there, Judy Billings was behind me. Like a miracle, the pain in my thumb disappeared.

For me, there was no such thing as pain when Judy Billings was around. I loved her. I was sure that any day she would start to love me back. In the meantime, she mostly ignored me.

But I kept trying. Judy was in the other fourth-grade class, so I didn't see too much of her. When I did, I figured I had to make the most of it.

That's why I held the door open for her. She went through. As usual, she ignored me. I didn't care. For one second, she was inches away. Heaven was a trainload of those seconds.

A little while later, during Silent Reading, a spider crawled onto Becky Hibble's book. Becky screamed and flipped her book into the air. The book landed on the floor. The spider landed in my lap.

Next thing I know, I'm on my desktop, tap dancing and yelling, "Get 'im off me! Get 'im off me!"

On the way to lunch, Joey's whisper came again: "Rats don't get scared of spiders."

We sat together in the lunchroom, just like last year. And we both brought our lunches from home, just like last year.

We sat at our usual table. I opened my lunch box. I was checking out my stuff when I heard Joey snickering. I looked up. He was wagging his head. His face was smirky.

I looked around the lunchroom. "What's funny?"

"That," he said. He was pointing at my lunch box.

"What's wrong with it?" I said.

"Ain't that the same one you had last year?"

"Yeah. So what?"

He snickered again. "Look at it."

I looked at it. "So?"

"What do you see?"

"I see a lunch box. What do you see, a Martian?"

He flipped the cover down. "*Look* at it. What's *on* it? All over it."

I looked again. "Elephants."

He broke out laughing. He pounded the table. His face was red. I had never known I could make him so happy. He tried to talk a couple times — "What — What —" but he kept cracking up. Finally he slapped his hand over his eyes and got it out: "What are they doing?"

"The elephants?"

"Yeah, yeah."

"They're flying."

This time I thought lunch would be over before he stopped laughing. Other kids were looking over. Gerald Willis, a sixth-grader and the school bully, threw a French fry at Joey, but that didn't stop him.

I unwrapped my sandwich. I didn't have all day.

At long last, he took a deep breath. He said, "Right. Flying elephants. Big flapping ears. Doing yo-yos with their trunks."

"*Some* of them," I corrected him. "Other ones have fishing poles."

His cheeks bulged with laugh balls, but he swallowed them.

"Morton —" He made himself serious. "Don't you get it?"

"Get what?"

"Flying elephants on your lunch box, man. That's little kiddie stuff." He picked up his paper bag. He wagged it in my face. "*This* is what a rat brings his lunch in."

I took a bite of my sandwich. "What do I care?"

"That's just it, man. You oughtta care." He opened his bag. "If you don't care, who will? Your mom probably got you that box, right?"

"Yeah, I guess."

"Right. Moms. They just want to keep you a baby all your life. Suds, I'm telling ya, you gotta put a stop to it now. If you leave it up to your mom, you'll be going off to college with a flying-elephant lunch box."

I looked at my lunch box. I'd had it since first grade, when I was a baby and glad of it. Most of the other kids broke their lunch boxes, or lost them, so they got new ones every year. My lunch box just kept rolling on. The elephants were fading, and some were even starting to look like hippos.

But I loved my lunch box. It was like a brother to me. Now that I thought about it, I wasn't even sure I could eat lunch at school without it. And as for my lunch box going off to college with me someday — well, to tell you the truth, I didn't see anything so bad about that.

I looked at Joey. He was wagging his head and smirking again.

Uh-oh, I thought, *it's not just the lunch box.*

ABOUT THE AUTHOR

Jerry Spinelli is the author of several novels, including *Third Grade Angels*, *The Library Card*, and *Maniac Magee*, which won the Newbery Medal. He lives in Wayne, Pennsylvania, with his wife and fellow author, Eileen Spinelli.

This book was designed by Kristina Iulo
and art directed by Elizabeth B. Parisi.
The text was set in New Century Schoolbook,
a typeface designed by Morris Fuller Benton
and Matthew Carter.
The book was printed
and bound at R. R. Donnelley in Crawfordsville, Indiana.
Production was supervised by Starr Baer,
and manufacturing was supervised by Adam Cruz.